W9-ATB-895

UNCORRECTED COLORPROOF

FROG, WHERE ARE YOU?

Sequel to A BOY, A DOG AND A FROG

by Mercer Mayer

THE DIAL PRESS   a pied piper book ®   New York

For Phyllis Fogelman,
a dear friend, who inspired
the creation of the faded
pink dummy.

FROG, WHERE ARE YOU?
is published in a hardcover edition by
The Dial Press, 1 Dag Hammarskjold Plaza, New York, New York 10017.
ISBN 0-8037-2729-1

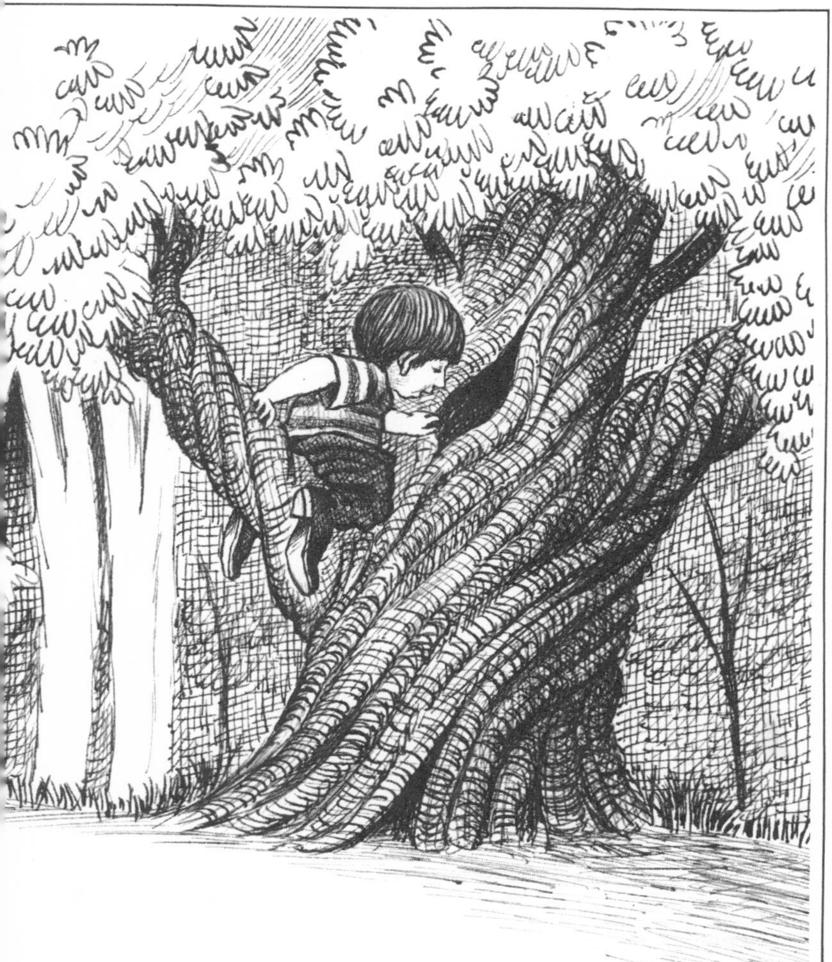